The
Best Traditional
Fairy Stories

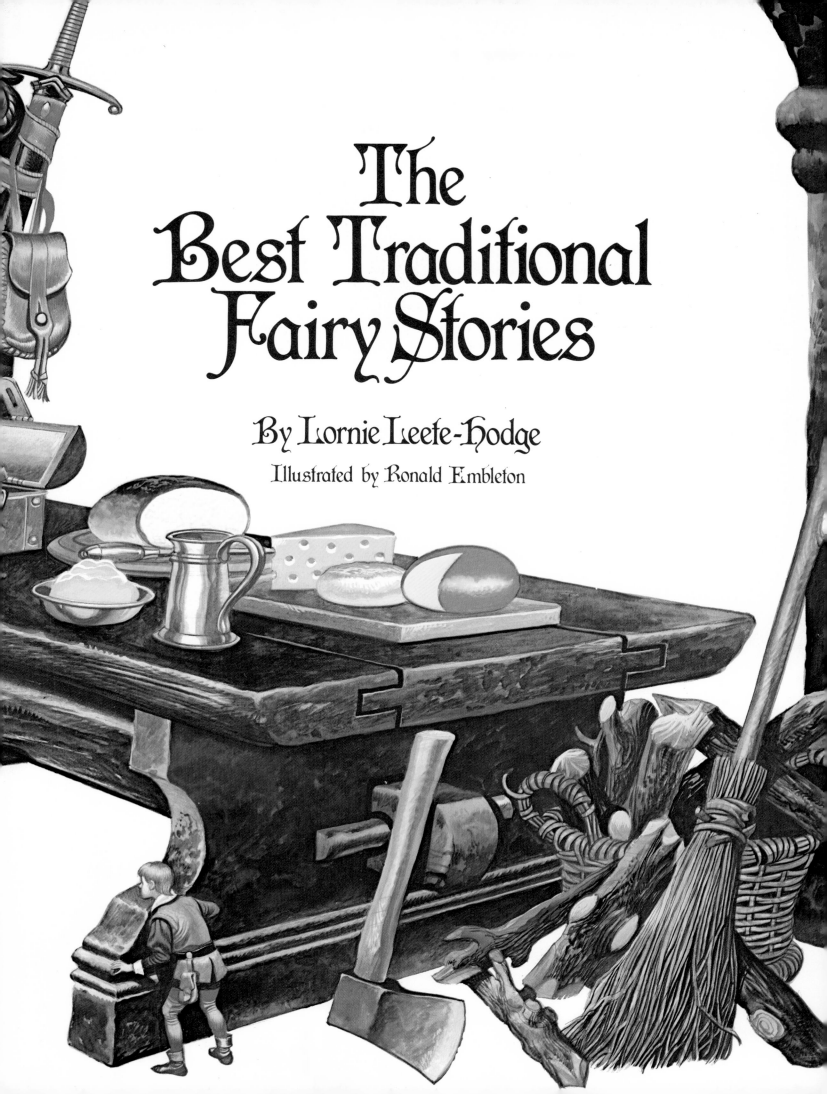

The Best Traditional Fairy Stories

By Lornie Leete-Hodge

Illustrated by Ronald Embleton

Originally published in England by Dean & Sons, Ltd.
Published in United States and simultaneously in Canada by Joshua Morris, Inc.
431 Post Road East
Westport, CT 06880
Copyright © The Hamlyn Publishing Group, Ltd. 1983
All Rights Reserved

ISBN 0-887-05058-1

Made and printed in Great Britain by
Purnell and Sons (Book Production) Ltd.,
Member of the BPCC Group, Paulton, Bristol

Contents

The Three Bears

Long, long ago, Three Bears lived together in a house deep in the forest. There was Father Bear who was big and tall, and spoke in a gruff, growly voice. There was Mother Bear who was smaller, with a softer, gentler voice and silky fur of which she was very proud. And, last of all, there was Little Bear who was very small, like a fluffy ball. His voice was rather more of a squeak!

The Three Bears were a happy family. Each bear's bed was different. Father Bear's was long and hard, he liked to feel a firm bed when he went to sleep. Mother Bear's was big, though not quite as big as Father Bear's, but it was quite different. Her bed was soft and full of feathers that sank down and covered her when she lay on it, just like a bird's wing. Little Bear had a small bed, which was not too big, not too small—not too hard and not too soft. In fact, it was just right—for him!

Father Bear had his own chair. This was very special. It was made of oak from the forest, and was big and strong, like him, and had its special place by the fireside. Mother Bear had a smaller chair, at the other side of the fireplace. This was softer with a big cushion for her to rest her back against when she sat by the fire. Little Bear had a small chair, that was not too big, not too small, but just right—for him!

The Bears' favourite food was porridge. When Mother Bear made it in the big pot on the stove, they all liked to stir it. Round and round, until it was smooth and creamy. Then, when it was steaming and ready, Father Bear would carry the pan very carefully to the table, and pour some into each bowl. He liked a lot, so he had the most. Not so much for Mother Bear, though she did not go hungry, and the last of the pan would go into Little Bear's bowl, with an extra spoonful of sugar on top, just as he liked it.

One fine morning, the Bears made the porridge as usual, but it was too hot to eat at once.

"Let's go for a walk while it cools," said Father Bear, and they all set off into the forest.

Now, they did not know it, but a little girl called Goldilocks, because she had such fair hair, was also walking in the forest. She had been told not to go far, but she loved to wander and soon was lost. She kept on along a little path until she came to the Bears' cottage.

"What a funny little cottage!" she cried, looking at it, with its crooked chimneys and thatched roof. She knocked at the door but there was no answer. So she peeped in at the windows. There, on the table, she could see three bowls, all steaming.

"Is anybody in?" she called out. No one answered. Goldilocks tried the door. It was open. So she went inside and looked around her. The three chairs stood near the fire. The table was set with three bowls, three spoons, one beside each plate, and a big jug of milk in the middle.

Goldilocks thought she would sit down. She climbed up into Father Bear's chair first.

"Oh, you are hard and horrid!" she said, jumping down.

Then she sat in Mother Bear's chair. "This is better," she said snuggling in, until she found the cushion in the way, and threw it on to the ground.

"This looks better!" she said and tried Little Bear's chair. But Little Bear was little and Goldilocks was much bigger, and soon there was a loud cracking sound! Little Bear's chair was in little pieces all over the floor.

"Oh dear me!" said Goldilocks getting up. She looked around. "I do feel hungry," she said, and she wandered over to the table and picked up the first spoon. She dipped it into Father Bear's porridge and had a taste.

"Ugh!" she cried, "you are too hot and too stodgy for me."

Next she picked up another spoon and tried Mother Bear's porridge.

"This is too cold and runny," she said and threw down the spoon.

Lastly, she picked up Little Bear's spoon and dipped it into his bowl.

"Oh, this is just right!" she said, "it's scrumptious!" And she ate every scrap, even scraping the bowl so as not to miss a bit.

"Ooh, now I feel tired," she said, yawning, and she looked around for somewhere to have a rest. She climbed up the little staircase. There was one big room with three beds set out in a row.

First of all there was the big bed that was hard and strong, just right for Father Bear. Next there was a smaller one, with a downy mattress

for Mother Bear, and at the end was the small bed where Little Bear slept. This had its very own bedspread with a row of little bears embroidered across it, which Mother Bear had made for him.

Goldilocks sat on Mother Bear's bed but found the feathers too hot and jumped off again. Then she came to Little Bear's bed. "How sweet," she said, folding back the bedspread with the bears. Soon she was between the sheets and fast asleep. She snuggled down. This was a lovely bed!

9

After a while, the Three Bears came home. As soon as he opened the door, Father Bear knew someone had been in. The place looked different.

"Mummy, look!" cried Little Bear in his squeaky voice. "Someone has been sitting on my chair. And it's all broken!" He began to cry.

"Someone's sat on my chair too," said Father Bear looking very cross. "And mine," said Mother Bear, "look, they have thrown my cushion on the floor!"

"Someone has been eating my porridge," said Father Bear. This was too much.

"And mine," said Mother Bear, "they have messed it all up!"

"But they have eaten every bit of mine," wailed Little Bear, crying again. It just wasn't fair. First his chair and now his lovely porridge.

"Let's go upstairs," said Father Bear. "They may still be there." So, one by one, and walking very softly, so as not to disturb anyone, the Three Bears went up the stairs. Father Bear threw open the door of the bedroom. The beds were all there in a row. He went to his bed.

"Someone has been sleeping in my bed!" he growled.

"Someone has been sleeping in my bed too!" said Mother Bear.

"Someone has been sleeping in my bed," squeaked Little Bear. "And," he squeaked louder in his excitement, "there is someone in my bed now!"

His voice woke Goldilocks who sat up in bed and rubbed her eyes. What a fright she had! Three Bears, looking very fierce were staring at her. She leapt out of bed and ran down the stairs as fast as her legs would carry her. She never once looked back. Never again did she venture into the forest. She was too afraid of meeting some more bears!

Poor Little Bear was very sad. Someone had eaten all his porridge, slept in his bed and broken his lovely chair. He began to cry.

"Never mind," said Mother Bear, putting her paw round him. "I'll make some more porridge, and when we have had a lovely breakfast, Daddy Bear will go into the woods and find some wood, and make you a lovely new chair. How about that?"

Little Bear clapped his paws. "Will you put my name on it so that everyone will know it is mine?" he asked.

And Father Bear promised to do just that. He often wondered who Goldilocks was, and what she was doing in the cottage, but he never said a word.

The Three Little Pigs

Once, long ago, there were three little pigs. When they were old enough to leave home, their mother sent them out into the world to seek their fortunes.

The eldest little pig set off along the road whistling a merry song. It was a sunny day, and he felt very happy. He was sure he would soon make his fortune. He'd show everyone how clever he was, he was the cleverest pig of all!

Soon he met a man carrying a load of straw.

"Will you sell me your straw for one penny?" he asked.

"What are you going to do with the straw?" asked the man.

"Why, I am going to build myself a fine house," replied the pig.

So the man sold him the straw and the little pig set off along the road once more to look for a place to build himself a house.

The second little pig was also trotting along the road. His little hoofs went knickety-knack, knickety-knack as he hurried on his way. Soon he met a man with a load of hazel twigs. Then he had an idea!

"Will you sell me your fine load of hazel twigs?" he asked, stopping the man.

"What do you want with my load of hazel twigs?" asked the man.

"Why, I shall build myself a fine house," replied the little pig.

"Oh well, suit yourself," said the man and sold him the hazel twigs.

With the twigs on his back, the little pig hurried along the road, his hoofs going knickety-knack, knickety-knack until he could find a place to build his house.

The smallest of the little pigs walked slowly along the road. He was thinking very hard. At last he met a man with a load of bricks, and he asked him if he would sell him the bricks.

"Why do you want my bricks then, little pig?" asked the man.

"I want to build myself a fine house," said the little pig. "I can pay you two whole pence for them."

"Agreed," said the man, and the little pig put the bricks on his shoulder and set off down the road.

Meanwhile, the first little pig had chosen a shady spot by the roadside, and was busy building himself a little house. He sang as he worked and thought himself very clever. It did not take him long to make his house and he was very proud of it. He walked up and down in the sunshine admiring it. Little did he know that a large grey wolf, hiding behind a tree, was watching him.

"Ho, ho, ho," said the wolf, "I'll soon have that pig!"

The second little pig saw his brother's straw house, and decided to make his twig house nearby. While his brother stood in the sunshine watching him, the second pig ran hither and thither, and soon his hazel twig house was finished. Then he stood in the doorway and waved to his brother in the straw house.

The smallest little pig was finding his load of bricks rather heavy so he found a spot very near the house of hazel twigs and began to build his house of bricks.

And the large grey wolf was still behind the tree, watching them!

The smallest pig toiled in the sunshine all day. Building a house was hard work but he did not stop until the last brick was in place. Then he went inside and shut the door. He felt hungry so he put a large pot on the fire to cook his supper. At last he could have a rest and put his little feet up. He was especially proud of his house. It had taken him a long time to make, but it was sturdy and solid. He felt safe as houses!

As dusk fell, the grey wolf slunk up to the eldest pig's house of straw. He knocked at the door.

"Let me in," he cried, "let me in, little pig."

"Oh no, Mister Wolf," cried the little pig, who had seen him through a crack in the straw, "I won't let you in."

"Well then," said the wolf,

"I'll huff and I'll puff,

"And I'll blow your house down."

And the little pig trembled as he huffed and he puffed, and the straw house began to shiver and shake. Soon, it would be all blown away. The little pig scrambled through a hole in the back and ran along the road to hide.

Soon, the house blew away and the wolf rushed in to eat the eldest pig. But there was no one there! Very angry, the wolf crept on until he came to the second pig's house of hazel twigs. Once again, he knocked softly at the door.

"Let me in, let me in, little pig," he called.

"Oh no, Mister Wolf," said the little pig who had seen him through the keyhole. "I won't let you in—not ever!"

"Well then," said the wolf,

"I'll huff and I'll puff,

"And I'll blow your house down."

And he huffed and he puffed. The hazel twig house stood firm. So he tried again, harder and harder, until the hazel twigs began to crackle and shake. Soon they all began to move. The terrified little pig ran out at the back, and hid with his elder brother. They watched as the hazel twig house blew away into the forest and the wolf stood there, his jaws slavering, and his eyes glinting. The pig had gone!

The two little pigs did not wait to see any more! They ran and ran until they came to the brick house their little brother had built. He had seen them coming and opened the door.

"Quick!" he said, "lock the door behind you! We must keep the wolf out."

So the three little pigs waited for the wolf to come. He was so angry he did not tiptoe to the front door. He banged loudly and called out to the pigs, "Little pigs, open the door!" They did not answer.

"All right," said the wolf.

"I'll huff and I'll puff,

"And I'll blow your house down."

So he huffed and he puffed. Nothing happened. He tried again. He huffed and he puffed. He puffed and he huffed. Nothing moved the brick house. Angrily the wolf slunk away.

Next day the little pigs danced and sang in the brick house. Then they heard the wolf calling.

16

"Little pigs, little pigs," he said in a soft voice. "I know where there are some fine turnips in Mr Brown's field. Be up at six and I will show you where they are!" And he went off chuckling.

But the youngest little pig got up at five and found the turnips in Mr Brown's field and brought them back to his house. When the wolf called to him at six, he called back, "I know about the turnips, they are in my pot!"

The wolf went off. Later he came back again. "Little pigs," he called, "how would you like some rosy apples?"

"Yes please," said the little pigs.

"Well come with me at five, and I will show you the tree," said the wolf. He knew the pigs loved apples. This time he would not miss!

But the youngest little pig was up at four and gathered all the

17

apples! When the wolf called out at five, he said, "Yes I know all about the apples. Would you like to try one?" He threw him an apple.

All day the wolf paced up and down in a rage. Somehow, somehow he must get in to eat those succulent little pigs! Then he had an idea!

At night, while the pigs were sitting round the fire, the youngest pig held up his foot. "Shush," he whispered, "Listen!"

All was quiet. Then the little pig heard the sound again. It was coming from above him. Then he knew. The wolf was on the roof!

"Quick," he said, "put all the wood you can on the fire! Pile it on to make it blaze." And he lifted up a big black pot full of water and put it on top of the flames. Soon it was boiling merrily!

Scrape, scrape, scrape, the wolf crept nearer and nearer along the roof and then he called down the chimney, "Little pigs, little pigs," he shouted. "I am coming in to gobble you up!" And he slid down the chimney.

Just as he reached the bottom, the little pig lifted the lid off the pot and the wolf fell into the boiling water! That was the end of him! But the little pigs lived happily in the brick house, and danced and sang in the sunshine.

Jack and the Beanstalk

A poor widow lived alone in a little cottage with her son, Jack. He was a kind and happy boy, but a lazy one, who did nothing to help his mother.

The day came when there was no money in the house. Though she turned out every cupboard, and looked under every board, the widow could not find a single coin.

"Oh, dearie me!" she exclaimed, "Whatever shall we do?" And she wrung her hands in misery. Then she had an idea. "There's only one thing for it," she said, "Daisy will have to go to market."

"But, Mother," said Jack, "Daisy's been our cow for years and years!"

"I know, and I shall miss her. But what else can I do? You must take her to market in the morning."

So Jack's mother gave Daisy a special feed that night, and he helped her to polish her hoofs until they shone. Daisy must look her best next day.

"Mind you get a good price for her," said his mother as Jack set out leading Daisy by a long rope.

Jack did not hurry. It was a nice day and he felt very proud to be going to market on his own, even if he was sorry to say goodbye to Daisy. He might buy himself some sweetmeats at the market. His eyes lit up and his step quickened.

All at once, a strange man came alongside him.

"Good morning, young sir," he said, "where are you going?"

"I'm going to market to sell this fine cow," said Jack. "She's called Daisy."

"No need to go to market," said the man. "I want to buy a cow, and Daisy will do me very nicely. I'll give you these five magic beans. If you plant them, they will make you very rich."

Jack did not hesitate. He took the beans in their little brown bag, patted Daisy on the head and told her to be a good girl. Then he ran all the way home, the beans rattling in the bag with every step.

"Mother! Mother!" he called. "I'm back and I've sold Daisy!"

"My! That was quick," said his mother, drying her hands on a cloth. "Well, did you run all the way to market? It's a fair step to be back so soon."

"No, I never even went to market," Jack told her. "I met this man on the road, and he bought Daisy."

"Well, what price did you get? I hope you didn't let her go cheaply."

"Look, Mother, the man gave me these magic beans for Daisy," Jack began to explain, but his mother cut him short.

"You stupid boy!" she said and boxed his ears. "You have sold Daisy for a bag of worthless beans! Whatever will become of us?"

And she tossed the beans out of the window and sent Jack to bed without any supper. How could he have been so silly?

Jack was so hungry, for he had had no supper, he woke early the next morning. The sun was shining, but what a surprise he had when he looked out of the window!

In the middle of the garden, where his mother had thrown the bag of beans, was a huge plant, its leaves as big as plates.

"Mother!" Jack called, "Come and see!" And they both went out into the garden to stare. Neither of them had ever seen such a plant. It went up and up and up and up, until it seemed as if the top would reach the sky.

"Jack, come back!" his mother called, but her son had his foot on the lowest branch and was climbing higher and higher, until he was soon out of sight.

After a while, Jack stopped to have a breather. Climbing was hard work in the sun. He looked down and could see, far, far below him the roof of his home. How small it looked! He looked up and saw that the plant seemed to be reaching up to the fluffy clouds in the sky.

At last Jack came to the end of the branches and stepped off into a huge field. In the distance he could see a castle, so he made his way towards it, and knocked on the door.

He did not know it, but a fierce ogre lived there. His wife opened the door an inch and peered out. "What is it?" she said.

"Please may I have a drink of milk?" asked Jack for he was very thirsty and hungry.

"Come in," said the old woman, and gave him some milk and a piece of bread. Jack was famished, and ate happily.

"Hurry up," said the old woman, her head on one side, as if she was listening.

"What is it?" asked Jack, his mouth full.

"My husband is coming back," said the old woman. "He mustn't find you here," and she pushed Jack into a huge oven.

Thump! Thump! Bump! The very floor shuddered and Jack, in the oven, wondered what was happening. It sounded like an earthquake!

The ogre, the biggest man you have ever seen, with dark brown hair and whiskers, and thick, thick arms and legs, came stamping into the room. He looked all round him and sniffed. Then he began to shout,

"Fee, fi, fo, fum,

I smell the blood of an Englishman.

Be he alive or be he dead,

I'll grind his bones to make my bread."

"Oh, hush," said his wife. "Eat your breakfast. It's all ready for you."

Soon the only sound was the giant eating and drinking. He ate three whole lambs, ten loaves of brown bread, washed down with a gallon of ale.

"Ah! that's better," he said, wiping his mouth. "Now bring me the hen that lays the golden eggs," he ordered and sat back in his huge chair.

"Lay," he ordered when the hen was set before him. The hen laid a golden egg. Then another and another and another. Soon a dozen shining golden eggs lay on the table. The ogre put them all in a basket. Then, feeling sleepy, he lay back in his chair and soon the room shook to the sound of his snores.

Jack, who had peeped out of the oven when he saw the hen, crept out and tiptoed past the sleeping giant. Then, quick as he could, he picked up the hen, and pushing it under his arm, ran as fast as his legs would carry him back to the beanstalk. Just as he reached it, the hen began to cackle, and Jack could hear the giant running behind him. But quickly he slid down the beanstalk and ran to his mother.

At first she did not believe his story of the ogre and the castle and the magic hen. She was glad they had a hen at all!

"Lay," Jack ordered the hen, setting it on the table. The hen laid a golden egg.

"Lay another," said Jack again. And so it went on until they had so many eggs they did not know what to do.

Jack and his mother had plenty of money now, and wanted for nothing, but Jack soon grew bored and wanted to climb the beanstalk once more.

This time Jack ran to the castle but did not knock on the door in case he met the ogre's wife. He climbed in an open window and hid behind a milk churn. He had not long to wait. Once again, the giant came into the house and the whole building shook with every step he trod. He looked more frightening than ever, and Jack crouched lower.

"Fee, fi, fo, fum,

I smell the blood of an Englishman.

Be he alive or be he dead

I'll grind his bones to make my bread,"

roared the giant again. He looked all round the room, but Jack kept out of sight.

"Come along and eat your supper," said his wife, "it's some beef, cooked the way you like it."

Jack watched as the giant ate plate after plate of beef, the fat running down his whiskers, washed down with foaming ale. At last he had had enough.

"Bring me my gold, so that I may count it," he ordered, and his wife brought him two sacks that chinked and jingled as he tipped them out on to the table.

First of all, the ogre ran his great hands through the gold pieces, lifting them up and laughing as they fell. He loved his money. Then he began to count it, making first one pile, then another, and another, and another, until the whole table was stacked with gold. Tiring of this, the ogre sat back in his chair and fell asleep, his snores blowing the curtains at the other side of the room.

Quickly, Jack stepped out from behind the milk churn. He picked up a money bag and filled it with gold pieces until he could carry no more. Then he ran, as fast as his legs would carry him until he reached the beanstalk. There was no sign of the giant, but Jack did not wait, and slid down to the bottom. His mother was very pleased with all the gold pieces, and told him not to go up the beanstalk ever again.

Time passed and Jack would look up at the beanstalk and long to climb it, just once more. At last he could bear it no longer, and climbed up quickly one morning before his mother saw him.

This time he slipped in the door which stood open and was just in time to hide behind a chest when the giant came in. He was even bigger than Jack remembered!

"Fee, fi, fo, fum,
I smell the blood of an Englishman.
Be he alive or be he dead
I'll grind his bones to make my bread."
The giant was in full voice. He looked all around him and sniffed, but he did not see Jack.

"Come along," said his wife, "I've ten fine turkeys for you to eat, roasted to a turn."

And Jack watched as the giant ate first one, then another and another of the crisp turkeys until there was nothing left but a pile of bones. Once again he lay back in his chair. "Fetch my harp," he ordered his wife, "it can play us a tune until I feel sleepy."

So the ogre's wife fetched a beautiful golden harp which she set on the table. Soon, by magic, it began to play the most soothing music Jack had ever heard. How his mother would love it! Before long both the ogre and his wife were fast asleep. Jack crept from his hiding place

and picked up the harp and ran out of the castle. As he reached the door, the magic harp called out to the ogre. "Master! Master!" And the ogre woke up with a start.

Jack sped across the fields and he could hear the ogre close behind him. His legs had never run faster. But the ogre was getting nearer and nearer!

As he reached the beanstalk, Jack could see the ogre a few yards behind him.

"Stop!" he bellowed. "Come back here!"

But Jack slid down the beanstalk as if it was slippery! "Mother! Mother!" he called, "bring me an axe. Hurry!"

For the ogre was already on the beanstalk which was swaying to and fro with his weight.

Jack seized the axe and began hacking at the beanstalk with all his might. He could see the ogre just above him! There was no time to lose.

With a great cracking, rending sound, the beanstalk began to break. Then with a mighty swish! it fell to the ground, the ogre clinging to its branches. It was so long it seemed to stretch for miles, but there was no sign of the ogre. No one ever saw him again.

Next day the magic beanstalk had all disappeared. Some dried beans lay on the path and Jack's mother put them in a jar—for safekeeping, and she and Jack lived happily ever after.

Beauty and the Beast

Long ago and far away, there lived a rich merchant who had three daughters. They were all beautiful, but the youngest was by far the loveliest, and was always known as Beauty. This made her sisters jealous, especially as she was her father's favourite. The merchant gave his children everything they could wish for, and they lived in luxury.

Then, suddenly his luck changed and the merchant had very little money. He had to sell his fine house and take his daughters to live in a little cottage in the country.

As they were poor, all three had to work hard. The two elder sisters grumbled all day, but Beauty sang while she worked. As long as her family was together, she was happy.

One morning, the merchant had good news. One of his ships had come home with riches from the East. He hurried to meet the ship at the port.

"I can bring you all presents, my children," he said smiling. "What would you like?"

"Oh Father, please bring me a sapphire and diamond necklace," said the eldest daughter. She loved fine jewellery.

"Father I would like a red dress with white lace on the collar," said the second daughter who loved fine clothes. "Don't forget the lace," she told him.

"I'll remember," laughed the merchant. "And what about you, Beauty, what shall I bring for you?"

"Father, I should like a red rose better than anything else," said Beauty.

So the merchant rode off to the port. But when he arrived, he found his goods had been stolen. So he had no money after all. There was nothing to do but return home. With a heavy heart, he set out along the road. What could he tell his daughters?

As he rode along, hunched in misery, the merchant noticed that snow was falling. Soon, it would be too thick for him to go on. He must find shelter. Snow lay all around him and night was coming on. He could hear the wolves howling, but there was no shelter.

Suddenly, he found himself in an avenue of orange trees, sweet smelling and green. At the end was a huge castle. Very surprised the merchant hurried along to seek shelter in the great house. Though the mangers were full, there were no horses, nor did anyone answer when he pulled the bell. The door was open, so he went inside. Everything was very rich, with fine rooms and bright fires burning in the firegrates. Gratefully, the merchant held out his hands to the fire. At last, tired out and warm, the merchant fell asleep.

When he awoke, hours later, the fire had been made up, and a little table had been laid beside him, filled with food. It must be meant for me, thought the merchant, and ate a good meal. It was all very strange!

Later the merchant wandered through the rooms, each one more magnificent than the last, but he saw no one. In the garden, it was as if it was midsummer with the birds singing, the flowers sweet smelling, and the bees buzzing lazily above.

Then the merchant remembered his promise to Beauty. He saw a bush full of the most beautiful, sweet-smelling roses he had ever seen, and leaned forward to pick one. At least he could bring Beauty a present if he had nothing for the other girls.

"How dare you!" The merchant jumped. A fierce voice spoke behind him, and he turned, the rose in his hand.

"Who said you might gather my roses?" asked a terrible voice, and he saw a terrifying Beast towering above him, with horns and great huge paws from which sheathed claws grabbed at him.

The poor merchant dropped the rose and fell to his knees.

"How dare you steal!" thundered the Beast. "I have saved your life, let you sleep in my house, given you food, and now you steal my roses. No one steals my flowers and lives. You must die!"

"Oh, forgive me," begged the merchant. "I am truly grateful that you saved my life and gave me food. I looked all round to thank you, truly I did."

"Well, why did you steal *my* rose?" the Beast asked again.

"Let me explain, I beg of you," pleaded the merchant. He told the Beast his story, and how, though he could not give the elder girls their jewels and clothes, he could keep his promise to Beauty.

The Beast looked at him. At last he growled, "Well, I will forgive you—but on one condition. You must give me one of your daughters."

"Oh have mercy!" begged the merchant, but the Beast would not listen.

"One month from now," he said, "you must bring one of your daughters to me. And she must come of her own free will. If she does not come, you will die."

And the Beast disappeared. The merchant found his horse saddled and waiting in the courtyard, with a chest of gold and jewels strapped to its back. A fresh rose lay in a silk scarf.

When he came home the merchant's daughters were waiting.

"Did you bring my necklace, Father?" asked the eldest, kissing him.

"And my dress, the one with the lace collar?" asked the second.

Beauty just kissed him. "Welcome home, Father," she said.

"Beauty, here is your rose," he said, handing it to her and she clapped her hands in delight. "Where did you find such a rose? I have never seen one like it. Oh, thank you, dear, dear Father!"

But the merchant shook his head in sorrow. Later, as they sat round the fire, he told them of all that had befallen him on his journey.

"What shall I do?" he asked them. "What shall I do?"

"Never fear, dear Father," said Beauty. "As it was for me you stole the rose, and the Beast was angry, it is only right that I should go and live with him. Do not be afraid."

All too soon, the month passed and the merchant knew he must take Beauty to live with the Beast. Sorrowfully, he helped her to pack her clothes and they set off on the horse that her father had brought home.

No sooner were they on the road than it all changed! And, because it was a magic horse, it took them to the Beast's castle. Light shone from every room, and soft music floated out into the gardens. Once again, there was no sign of the Beast, but everything was ready for Beauty.

"What a lovely place!" Beauty cried as she and her father went from room to room. At last they sat down to eat. Then they heard the Beast's footsteps coming along the passage, and Beauty clung to her father in terror.

"Good evening," said the Beast. "Is this Beauty who has come to live with me?"

"I am Beauty," she said timidly, still holding her father's hand.

"Welcome," said the Beast. "Will you stay here when your father leaves?"

Beauty could hardly speak for fear, but she gulped back a sob. "Yes," she whispered, "I will stay with you."

Next morning, the merchant left with presents of fine dresses and jewels for her sisters. Beauty tried hard not to cry when he rode away, but she felt very much alone and afraid.

She went to her room and cried herself to sleep. As she slept she dreamed that sweet music was playing and a soft voice was saying, "Do not cry, Beauty, all will be well."

Next morning Beauty was awakened by the sweet sound of a clock that chimed her name a dozen times. She found the cupboards full of clothes and everything she could want, and, when she had dressed, she went downstairs to have breakfast.

A meal was ready for her but there was no sign of the Beast. When she had finished Beauty decided to explore the castle, going from room to room, wondering at the lovely things she found. The first room was lined with mirrors and Beauty danced up and down watching her

skirts swirl. Soft music began to play and her steps got quicker and quicker in time.

"Oh!" said Beauty, "I'm breathless. I'll go into the garden for some air." And she wandered out into the garden, where a fountain played, and the bees buzzed and birds sang. There was no sign of the Beast.

Beauty wandered on and on and came to the lovely rose bush from which her father had plucked the rose for her. She buried her face in the blooms, "When shall I ever see you again?" she whispered and her eyes filled with tears.

Later, she found another meal waiting for her. All her favourite food on tiny, china dishes was spread out on a snowy cloth. There was no sign of the Beast.

So the days passed, and Beauty walked in the gardens, played the tiny piano she found in one of the rooms, or read one of the books that lined the shelves. To her delight, every book had her name in it. How thoughtful the Beast was, she said to herself. Everything was for her happiness!

That evening, when she had eaten, the Beast came to sit with her. Beauty tried not to show her fear.

"Are you happy, Beauty?" he asked gruffly.

"Oh yes, you have been very kind," Beauty told him.

"Do you like living here?" he asked her.

Beauty hesitated. She was not unhappy. She just wanted to be at home with her father and sisters.

The Beast shook his head sorrowfully and went away.

A few days later he asked her again if she was happy, and she told him she liked the castle.

"Will you marry me?" he asked softly.

"Oh no, Beast," said Beauty, "I could never marry you."

"Very well," he said sadly, and walked away.

Beauty was glad she had not made him angry when she refused him. She was still a little afraid of him, though he did all he could to please her. It was just that she wanted so much to go home.

One night the Beast asked her, "Do you find me so ugly then, Beauty? Will you ever marry me?"

And she told him, "No, you are not so ugly. But I can never marry you!"

As time went on Beauty grew more and more homesick. She longed to see her father and sisters once more and felt she could not bear it. One morning she found a ring on her table with a message:

YOU MAY GO HOME FOR A VISIT. BUT YOU MUST COME BACK IN TWO MONTHS OR I SHALL DIE. PUT THE RING ON THE TABLE AND YOU WILL RETURN TO ME. DO NOT STAY TOO LONG FOR I CANNOT BEAR IT.

Next day Beauty woke up to find herself at home with her family, the ring on her finger. Oh, how happy she was to be at home again! The Beast had sent gifts of jewels and gold for her sisters and father, and everyone was very pleased to see her. The days flew and Beauty knew it was time to go back to the Beast.

That night she had a dream. She dreamed the Beast was ill and lying all alone on a bank pining for her. She knew she must return at once!

She said goodbye to her father and sisters and laid the ring on the table. Then at once she was back in the castle of the Beast. Quickly she ran up the steps. Suddenly, she wanted to see him again. She had missed the Beast!

"I'm here, Beast!" she called. "Where are you?"

But there was no sign of the Beast. She ran from room to room calling to him, but he did not answer. Then she noticed the beautiful furniture was dusty, the mirrors no longer sparkled. Everything was neglected as if the life had left it.

Distracted, she ran into the garden calling, "Beast, Beast, where are you? I've come home!" But there was no answer.

At last she found him lying on a bank under the big red rose tree she loved so much. She ran up to him and shook him. "Beast, Beast, I've come back!" But he did not answer.

Beauty took his head in her arms and stroked it. "Poor, dear Beast," she whispered, "don't die. I love you so. Oh, dear Beast," and she kissed him.

A faint voice asked her, "Will you marry me?"

This time Beauty did not hesitate. "Yes, dear Beast, I will marry you, for I love you so!"

But before Beauty could draw breath, Beast had turned into a handsome Prince, who held her in his arms as if he would never let her go.

Beauty laughed and cried and laughed again. "Oh Beast, what a fright you gave me! I thought you were dead."

"Oh my Beauty, I was very ill. If you had not come back when you did, I should have died," said the Beast.

And he told her how a wicked fairy had cast a spell on him when he was a boy. He had turned into a Beast spurned by all, and he would remain a Beast until someone who was beautiful told him she loved him and would marry him.

Beauty hugged him again. She had grown to love the Beast and how happy she was that he was really a Prince!

Idle Jack

A boy called Jack once lived with his mother in a little hut on a lonely moorland. His mother was very poor, and made some money by spinning. Jack was a big, strong lad, but he was too lazy to do anything to help. In the summer he lay out in the soft heather and gazed at the cloudless sky above him. In the winter he sat huddled by the fireside. He never went out at all!

"I've had enough of you!" his mother said one morning. "I can't bear you sitting around all day doing nothing. Be off with you!"

"Oh Mother," Jack said, "give me a chance! I'll get a job, really I will. See, you'll be proud of me."

"Well, see that you do then," his mother said. "Off to work on Monday, my lad."

Jack sulked all the weekend, but on Monday his mother pushed him out of the door.

A kindly farmer took pity on Jack when he found him wandering in his yard.

"I'll give you some work," he said, "you can take care of the sheep. I'll give you sixpence for it."

So Jack watched the sheep all day, and the farmer gave him six pennies.

Jack had never seen pennies before so he did not know what they were. On the way home, he jumped over a brook and the money dropped into the water, and he never saw it again.

"You stupid boy!" said his mother when he told her. "You must put anything you earn in your pocket!"

"I'll try," mumbled Jack. It was all very confusing.

On Tuesday Jack went to work for another farmer, who asked him to pour the milk into jugs for him. At the end of the day he gave Jack a jug of milk in payment.

Remembering what his mother said, Jack put the jug of milk in his pocket. As he ran home, the jug slipped, and all the milk spilt over his clothes!

"You are in a mess!" said his mother. "You've wasted a whole jug of good milk. You stupid, stupid boy! Next time, carry it on your head!"

"All right, Mother," said Jack, he couldn't do anything right.

The farmer gave Jack another job next day and gave him a pound of cream cheese as payment. Jack was going to put it in his pocket when he remembered his mother's words, and put it on top of his head.

As he ran home, the sun beat down and the cheese melted, and all he had to show for his work was a head full of cream cheese!

"What shall I do with you?" wailed his mother. "Go and wash your hair! You should have carried it in your hands! Remember in future."

So Jack left the farmer and went to work for a baker. The baker was a mean man. He soon saw how stupid Jack was, and gave him a spitting tom cat as his payment.

Poor Jack carried the spitting, scratching cat in his arms all the way

home. The cat struggled and squirmed and bit Jack, so when he reached home he had to let it go. He had nothing at all.

"Oh, what next!" exclaimed his mother. "There you are, all scratched and sore, and a day's work and no pay. You should have tied a string to it and dragged it home with you."

Jack tried working for a butcher next day. He worked well and the butcher was so grateful he gave him a large leg of lamb to take home as payment. Jack, remembering what his mother had said, asked him for a piece of string. Very surprised, the kindly man gave him a ball of string. Jack tied one end to the joint of lamb, and, holding on to the other, dragged the meat behind him all the way home in the dust. When he got home, it was not fit to eat. His mother was so angry, she hit him.

"Don't you know *anything*?" she cried. "You should have carried it on your head, you stupid boy."

"I'll remember," said Jack. He could do nothing right.

Next morning Jack set out bright and early and went to work for a herdsman. It was very tiring. At the end of the day the herdsman was pleased with Jack.

"You've done well, my lad," he said, "take this young donkey home with you as your wages."

So Jack thanked him and, remembering what his mother had said about the meat, lifted the donkey high, and put it on his head. He held on tightly as the donkey tried to escape. It brayed, kicked its legs and struggled. Poor thing, it had never had such a bad time in its life!

In the town there lived a rich man who had a beautiful daughter. She could not speak. All day long she sat by the window and watched

everyone passing by. The doctors said if she could but laugh, her speech would come back. But no one made her laugh.

Then she saw Jack with the struggling donkey on his head. "Oh my!" she gasped and burst out laughing. She laughed and laughed and laughed as if she would never stop. Her father and mother ran into the room on hearing her. Whatever had happened?

"Have you ever seen anything so funny?" she gasped, tears trickling down her face. "Oh, I can't stop laughing!"

The rich man ran into the street and took Jack into the house. "I have promised that whoever made my daughter laugh could marry her," he told him.

Jack could not believe his good fortune. His mother had the last word. "I told you to go out and do some work," she said, "see what good luck it has brought you!"

The Gingerbread Man

Once upon a time there lived a little old woman and a little old man in a little old house. One day the old woman made a little man out of gingerbread. She cut him out from the dough which she smoothed with her wooden rolling pin, then she made him a tiny jacket from chocolate, with tiny bright yellow seeds for buttons.

"There, what a fine little man you are!" she said as she put him in the oven to bake. She felt very pleased with herself.

"What's that, Wife?" asked the old man.

"Just you wait and see," she told him, 'you'll have a surprise!"

"Oh, you know I hate surprises, I'm too old for them," the old man said. "Come on, what's the mystery?"

"Well, as you won't wait, I've made a little gingerbread man for our very own," said his wife. "He's cooking in the oven at this very minute."

"Some surprise," grunted the old man. "You know I don't like gingerbread."

"Wait and see," said his wife, looking at the clock. She must not let the gingerbread man get too hard.

At long, long last, he was cooked and the old woman opened the door. What a fine little man he was! She felt so proud of him.

"Come and see," she called to her husband.

But before he could do so, the little Gingerbread Man suddenly jumped up, and ran away as fast as his legs would carry him!

"Hey! Wait!" shouted the old man and the old woman. "Come back here!"

But the little Gingerbread Man ran on and on. And the old man and the old woman ran down the street calling after him. The little Gingerbread Man shouted over his shoulder,

"Run! Run! As fast as you can!

You can't catch the Gingerbread Man!"

And they could not catch him.

He ran on and on until he came to a field. A cow looked over the gate at him.

"Stop, little Gingerbread Man," she mooed, "I would like to eat you."

But the little Gingerbread Man only laughed and ran on, calling out,

"Run! Run! As fast as you can!

You can't catch the Gingerbread Man!"

So the cow stopped munching the green grass in the field, and ran out of the gate after the little Gingerbread Man. But she could not catch him.

At last the little Gingerbread Man came to a horse who was looking out of a stable.

"Hey! Stop," neighed the horse, "I'd like to eat you."

But the little Gingerbread Man laughed louder and ran on, calling out as he went,

"I have run from an old woman,

And an old man,

And I can run away from you, I can! I can!"

And however hard the horse tried, he could not catch the little Gingerbread Man.

Some men haymaking in a field, heard all the noise and, laying down their pitchforks, came to see what was happening. When they saw the little Gingerbread Man, they, too, wanted to eat him. "Stop," they shouted, "wait for us! We want to eat you!"

But he only laughed and shouted to them.

"I have run from an old woman,

And an old man,

And a cow,

And a horse,

And I can run from you, I can! I can!"

So the haymakers joined in the chase. Everyone ran on and on down the long, long road. And the little Gingerbread Man turned round to them shouting,

"Run! Run! As fast as you can!

You can't catch the Gingerbread Man!"

So he ran on past a field of potato pickers who left their sacks and joined in the race, calling out to him to stop.

Once more he laughed at them and shouted,

"I have run from an old woman,
And an old man,
And a cow,
And a horse,
And some haymakers,
And I can run from you, I can! I can!"
However hard they ran the potato pickers could not catch him.

On and on ran the little Gingerbread Man, across the fields, and up hill and down dale. He met a red fox trotting across one field. As soon as he saw him the fox began to run, but the little Gingerbread Man shouted to him.

"I have run from an old woman,
And an old man,
And a cow,
And a horse,
And some haymakers,

And some potato pickers,

And I can run from you, I can! I can!"

The fox was close behind him when he called again.

"Run! Run! As fast as you can!

You can't catch me, the Gingerbread Man!"

But then he came to a river. He had never seen a river before and it scared him a little. He knew he could not swim across it. What could he do? He wanted to keep on running away from the old woman, the old man, the cow, the horse, the haymakers, the potato pickers and now the fox. He stopped at the edge and dipped his foot in the water. It was cold and flowing so fast, he knew he could not get over.

"Jump on my tail and I'll take you across," said the fox, "I can swim."

So the little Gingerbread Man jumped up on to the fox's tail. He held on very tightly and the fox began to swim across the river. When he was a little way across, he called out to the little Gingerbread Man.

"You are too heavy for my tail. I fear I shall drop you. Jump up on my back. You will be safer there."

So the little Gingerbread Man jumped on to his back. He held on very tightly to the fox's thick fur.

They had not gone many yards when the fox called out again. "I think the water is too deep. You will be covered. Jump up on my shoulder. You will be safer there."

So the little Gingerbread Man jumped up on to the fox's shoulder and held on ever so tightly. He did not want to fall off.

In the middle of the river, the fox called out to him once more. "Oh dear, my shoulder is sinking, and you will drown. Jump on my nose. You will be dry there."

So the little Gingerbread Man jumped up on to the fox's nose. It was slippery and he nearly fell, but he held on very tightly. It was very tickly and the fox's whiskers made him want to sneeze, but he held on.

As soon as the fox's paws touched the shore, he threw back his head and his jaws went snap!

"Oh dear!" wailed the little Gingerbread Man, "I am a quarter gone."

The next minute he cried, "I am half gone!"

Crunch! And he called out, "Why, I am three-quarters gone!"

And after that the little Gingerbread Man never said another word. He was all gone.

As for the fox, he licked his lips!